BLOOD
SWEAT
TEARS
. . . LIVE

Maya Englehorn
Kate Westphal

We write because we live
Not because we are writers

some things are written to you
some for you
but some may just be meant
for other ears

Contents

BLOOD

Fighting,

fighting against the world,

against each other.

A jab here,

one there.

A drop of blood,

of me,

of another,

of something else.

When you throw the punches,
I have no choice but to ignore the sting.
You're just searching for a reason to hate me.
I won't let you have one.

what's the score
who's in the lead
what'd you get
who finished first
who's best

the questions
when do they stop?

the hustle
when does it end?

keeping up with the jones'
does it last forever?

how did friends turn to rivals
and cheerleading to scorekeeping

all to prove you're flying higher than the rest
stop finding your value in my failure

-turn comparison into comradery

you can't force me to respect you
let me like you
respect will follow

Do you actually think a meaningful
relationship will come from your
devilish cajoles to make us feel
tingles for a second? What do
you honestly expect? For us to
hand you our bodies to be returned
the next day like an overdue library
book? Like possessions you can
toss out once no longer fond of?

-HECK NO

I have an itch
That I've rubbed raw
Made a big deal of something small
Now instead of waiting for it to leave
I'll have a scar

you buried me alive
feelings and all
left the shovel
and turned on your heel

good thing you don't know
how powerful I am
how strong I am
how you may have hurt me
but you never tarnished my soul

I rose up
grabbed the shovel
dug myself out
brushed off the dirt
cleaned up the mess you made
and continued on my way

get over yourself
you no longer have the capacity
to hurt me

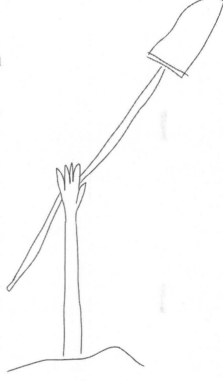

I want to slam the door right in your face
but if you knock I won't hesitate to open it
-mixed feelings

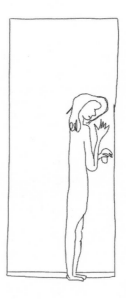

In sinking sand my childhood fear has come true
How did I get here
I didn't do the things I wasn't supposed to

So I thought of what
to do when going down, farther, farther, farther.
And then I did them.
Not struggle, not squirm, flail
Try to grab on to the
disappearing world.
helpless and alone.

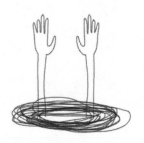

I hope that when you die
flowers grow from your compost
so I can say
something good came from you
without lying

He's not THE ONE, says my head.

 but he could be, says my heart.

It won't work and you know it.

 Is there harm in trying?

 No harm, but hurt.

 you're such a downer—don't you believe in love?

 you were right.

Don't be so sad.
EVEN YOU didn't really think it would work.

 i thought, but now I know it wasn't meant to last
 and somehow
 it's worse.

If I'm happy for you
it's harder to be hurt by you

The tension is palpable
Teeth grinding audible
Hurt feelings sickening
Unspoken words piercing

Yelling bubbling its way up
Doors about to be slammed
Exits about to be made
Tears about to be shed

Wine to drink
Kleenex to blow
But can't fix

-This family is toxic

I used to say you were the best thing that's ever happened to me.
We might not be close anymore,
but that hasn't changed.
You've taught me so much.
How to smile at a backstabber
How to be happy on your own
How to be peace in the storm
How to love the people that hurt you the most
How to provide your own joy
when your world has none

    -i thank you for that

plastic melts
water boils
wood burns
people shatter

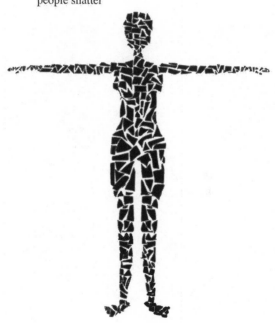

we see you
you know

how you jump from girl
to girl like stones across a
creek
rubbing the mud
from your shoes on our faces
only using us to stay out of the water

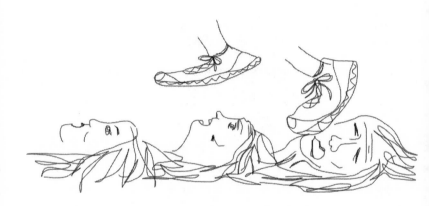

YOU FIERCE LITTLE FIGHTER
HAVE YOU EVER THOUGHT
ABOUT FIGHTING FOR SOMEONE
OTHER THAN YOURSELF?

You live on the surface
preoccupied with meaningless activities
following the leader
head in the sand
going through the motions
distracted
unappreciative
you've dipped your toe in
tried to get to me

But I'm too far below into what actually matters to hear you

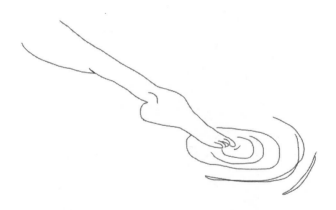

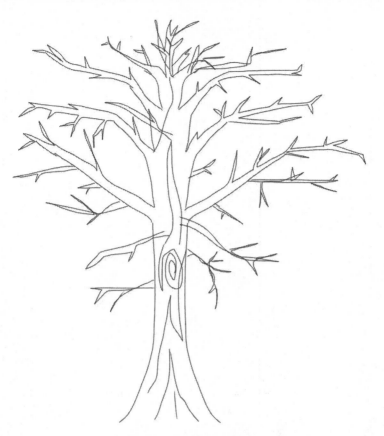

a tree produces its own seeds,
it provides everything it needs for the future.
But we are not producing seeds.
We are not preparing for our future.
We are destroying ourselves.
Our actions are reckless.
Life on earth is in a chokehold,
and we're the ones doing the choking.
We are injecting poison
in our own roots.
Setting fire to our branches
and watching ourselves burn.
We are committing an environmental suicide.

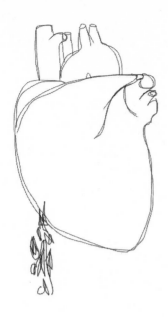

i can just feel the hate in my heart
weighing on me
you wouldn't notice
i try not to let it out
but if you look close
you can see it dripping
spilling out from a hole in my heart
a hole i am trying to cover up

-pain leaks

i tell myself i won't be your slave
just to be invited
but the comfort of being included
is stronger than the loneliness of begging

i don't see
why having values makes me boring
why i shouldn't live by my own standards
why i shouldn't follow my own moral compass
why i have to take your opinion to heart
sorry
i just don't understand
i don't want to

I wanted to figure this out together
But you brought an army and I came unprepared

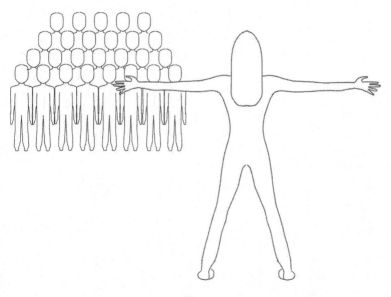

i'm attached to my old ways
there's a rope around my neck
connecting me
i pray it won't become a noose
and my habits
be the death of me

I guess families are for
Restarts and redoes
Forgive and forgets
But when is enough enough?

We need pain to give us a glimpse of hell,
Enough to make us crave heaven so much more.

I consider your opinions
do things the way you like
because I know and love you

but you continue to go blindly on
walking all over me with your opinions

never acknowledging my point of view
never considering I have one

you don't choose to know me
that's why I say
goodbye

Stop telling me
my thoughts are too
shallow

Do you know that I try?
Do you
even care?

How do you know
I'd rather just
not share?

I can think deep
just can't seem to
express

Can't put my thoughts
into phrases
Gosh darn

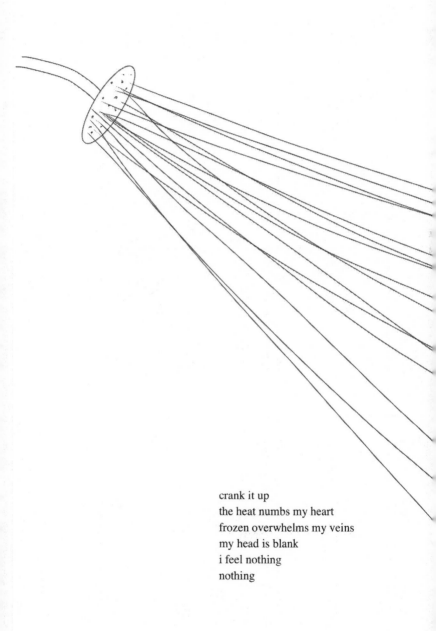

crank it up
the heat numbs my heart
frozen overwhelms my veins
my head is blank
i feel nothing
nothing

she sleeps, her eyes panicking in every direction beneath her lids.
a panic with skin, hiding it.
or maybe it's the other way around.
the skin is simply protecting from the panic outside

I had to pour salt
on the leech that
was sucking my blood
to save us both
the pain of the ripping

SWEAT

Product of toil, of worry,
of exhaustion, anticipation.
Of embarrassment, nervousness, or fear.
Uncontrollable response to surroundings.

I feel so out of control of my life
I don't know what to do
how I should feel
who I am
what I'm doing here

-who's driving?

I can feel the struggle between letting go and drowning
The hope and the stubborn
They are at war
and I don't know which one will win

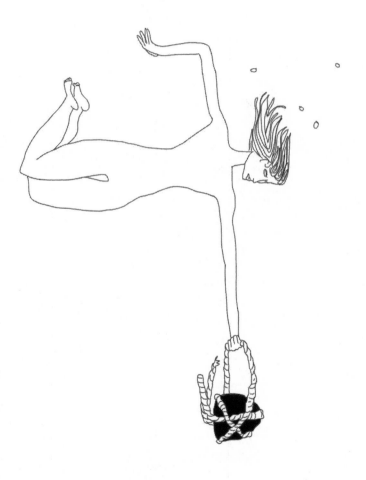

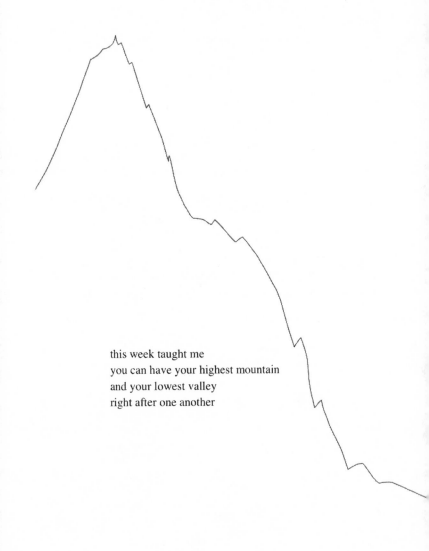

this week taught me
you can have your highest mountain
and your lowest valley
right after one another

At a low,
you can't help but wonder,
why me?
why not him?
i'm better than her.
The challenge is
to not question others success
when you haven't found yours yet.

Contradictions.
They are coming at me from all different sides.
Complications.
As if i don't have enough going through my head.

Depression & Anxiety
places all too familiar to us
places we're stuck - confused
glimmering darkness
deafening silence
lost where we can't see the stars
where there's no grip on the world
where we slide, slide farther down.
down until touch is cold and
familiar voices no longer draw us up.
that is the sensation -
cold and numb and careless

Why are we doing all this
so we can
get a job
and work
and get old?
Just to
make money?
Does life only get
worse from here?
There has to be more
God, show me what this life is all about

I'm worried
creativity leaving me
motivation saying goodbye
fears controlling me

I'm worried
I'm not all I should be
I don't amount

I'm worried
It's all purposeless
It's all for nothing

I'm worried
I'm right

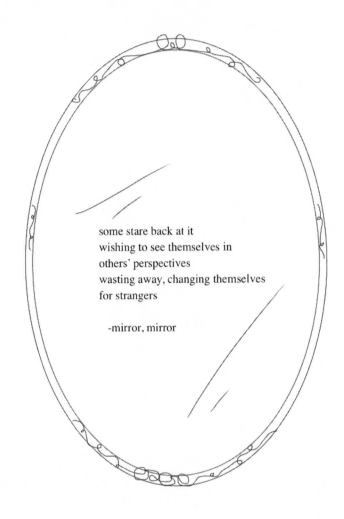

some stare back at it
wishing to see themselves in
others' perspectives
wasting away, changing themselves
for strangers

-mirror, mirror

i interact with
hundreds of people
thousands of personalities
millions of interests
some are total opposites
some hate each other
why do i want to be like all of them
 -conflicted

I'm afraid to write and be heard
to have my words used against me
thoughts twisted
ideas repurposed
misunderstood or interpreted

What if things are better left unsaid?

i'm a hot mess
a hurricane
a contradiction
i want to scream
cry
laugh
sing

i try to convince myself that
tomorrow will be better
everything will work out

but as far as i know,
there isn't one

 -hope is blind

When it's not quite theirs
They won't leave a mark
Stays clean inside and out
They won't take any risks
Damages are fixed
But if
It belongs to them
No matter if there's
scrape or dent or rust
When it starts to smell
oh well, whatever
No hurry to clean
and wash when it gets
them from place to place
It does the job there's
no need to look nice
registered under
their name.

Such a waste of air and
space
Watching others work and
create
Living, breathing, but not
thriving

-Is all I am alive?

you have so much in front of you
yet you reach for another branch.

white shoes
she wore white shoes in the mucky world
always hoped for the best
an idealist
but life moves fast
suddenly
everyone thinks she came unprepared
suddenly
it's uncool to be spotless
every direction she walks there is muck
she tries to hide that she's wholesome
but without any luck
some people think she's sensitive
even the ones who used to be clean have been sucked in
they tell her to grow up, it's life
but, she thinks, it won't be mine

the black shoes aren't what they seem.
on white shoes
what you see is what you get.
on black shoes
there's all sorts of darkness and evil.
you never know what's lurking behind
all that black.
what good are white shoes in a world of muck?

it's hard to see the rainbow
when you're standing in the rain
 -persist

my mind got put on hold
it knows it's meant for something great,
just waiting.
anxious.
in position.

life has a start buzzer.
get set,
ready for the go.

waiting for the world.
and i think it's waiting for me too.

 -ready to pounce

i feel like people know me
for my ideas and dreams
instead of knowing
me for me.

but maybe they're right
i'm nothing but dreams anyway.

WE WILL NOT BE ANOTHER STATISTIC
WE WILL NOT BE THE NEXT GROUP
DEVOTING OUR LIVES
ONLY TO DIE UNACCOMPLISHED
THE LADDER HAS BEEN BUILT FOR US
AND NOW IT'S OUR JOB TO
BREAK THE CEILING DOWN

-WOMEN'S RIGHTS ARE NOW

You care so much about being in the ins
That you leave everyone else in the outs
So self conscious
You are controlling
So discouraged
You are judgemental
All this pain that you have caused me
And I feel bad for you

i'm ready to jump
Lord
you have given me opportunities
opened all the doors
and here i am
with my feet glued to the floor
stuck in the hallway

There's an up and down to every hill.
There's a positive and negative to every situation.

    -Choose your angle

Dreams and Ambitions
but no idea what to do with them
not unplanned, entirely,
just thinking hard
weighing my options
measuring the risk
deciding what next

i keep
trying
&
trying
&
trying
but nothing ever works
it seems like you're resisting
but you'd say differently

if you don't separate yourself from unhealthy things
you'll become unhealthy yourself

-snip snip

reaching out my hand
and having it laughed at
puts kindness on the chopping block
not just me

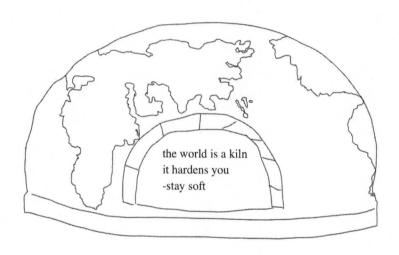

the world is a kiln
it hardens you
-stay soft

It's Saturday, but Sunday
will come and then Monday
with Friday night glimmering
in all eyes.
A lucky day, that Friday.
Nobody dreads Fridays.
Nobody blames their bad
moods on it.
Poor Mondays.
Can't anyone see there's
just as much opportunity
in a Monday?

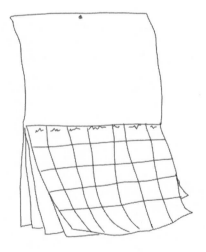

They told her to talk
When she does
They walk away

-What do you want?

Let's lock a girl in a cage
with her fears and anxieties
see how long it takes
for her to escape
and call it education

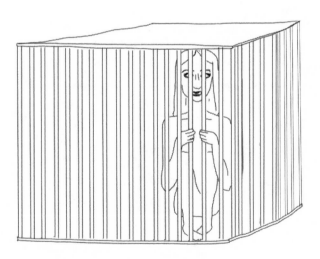

something is different
there's change in the air
i feel strange
out of place
i'm not the same anymore
the question is
am i finding myself
or losing myself?

i don't hate the silence

and you're the one who
makes it awkward.

creator of ugliness
of unproportional features
head scratching color schemes
bent straight lines
and flat circles
my artistic abilities irritate me

It's hard to see your accomplishments
when you never look back
-You've come so far

The obstacles thrown at me are
Almost as strong as
The urge to be better

don't invalidate your problems
just because someone has it harder than you.

-a struggle is a struggle

i guess a flame
as bright as us
was not meant to last

79

one of the worst things you can do
is to destroy someone's dream

-respect the dreamers

just because I want you
doesn't mean I need you

just because I have you
doesn't mean I'll keep you

-without you, I'm still me

Sacrifice

Who needs sleep she yawned
Who needs a shoulder she cried
Who needs a blanket she shivered
Who needs food she grumbled

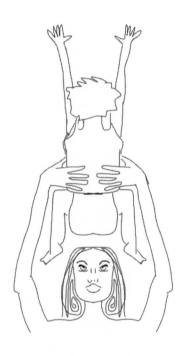

Stride reaching
Blood pulsing
Head rushing
Hands grasping
Arms pumping
Eyes searching
Mind focused

-the pursuit

I feel like wasted energy
What mountains have I moved
What cities have I powered
when I run
Is it all for nothing?

my body is the one true
thing that belongs
solely to me.

forgive me if I want
to keep it to myself
for a while longer.

Maybe my eyes are too small
and my feet too big

Maybe my hips are too wide
and my calves too thin

Maybe my hair is too flat
and my stomach too fat

Or maybe I judged too harsh
And have been beautiful
this whole time

She is stronger than everyone.
Because she has never given up on the world
even when the world
gave up on her.
She has never given in
and she never will.
She has never stopped trying to be good.

TEARS

Appears in the eyes,
but a true product of heart and soul and ache,
of reminisce and mistake

at rock bottom
dandelions don't grow
there's no room for wishes
no room for hope

melting into the background
hollowing yourself out
soon we will ask
are you there

Before I knew how to open the drain
I was drowning in my deepness
mouth pressed against the glass
for one last gasp
Suffocating myself with my own pain

-Unplug the drain

I haven't felt myself lately
Now I realize it's because
I don't have you anymore
How could I be myself
When part of me is missing

sitting there
at my breaking point
at my lowest
tears rolling down my cheeks
the sound of life filling up my emptiness
cars rushing by
life moving on
without me

It was like hot water over a fevering body
A rush of warmth to mask the chills
But no way to heal
No lemon-honey tea to fill a drained body
no bed to rest a heavy head
no arms to tuck the aching limbs
no lips to kiss the burning face
No one there to last

Just feel out
of place
right now

I am home
but not
welcome

Surrounded
but
alone

I fell in love with the idea of him
but I fell out of love with who he was
 -paying the price

Your friends don't know my name
Like we never even happened
But memories don't go away
Feelings just don't disappear
like the photos you deleted or the notes you ripped up.

-You can't erase me

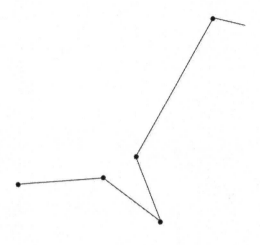

working on connecting
but it's the dots that I can't seem to find

I'm sure I've missed thousands of opportunities
to do great things
by a shake of my head
and a polite no thanks.

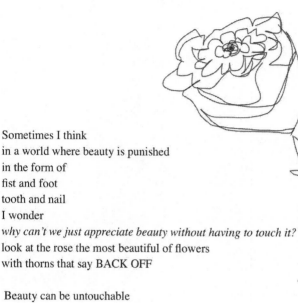

Sometimes I think
in a world where beauty is punished
in the form of
fist and foot
tooth and nail
I wonder
why can't we just appreciate beauty without having to touch it?
look at the rose the most beautiful of flowers
with thorns that say BACK OFF

Beauty can be untouchable

i don't miss you anymore
not because i don't love you
just that i've adjusted to life without you

my hate is numb
but so is my love
it's still there,
just lost somewhere

i'm fragile
i shudder at the suggestion of violence
at the sound of tears, i cry
i shrink from the first harsh word
at the sight of blood, i shriek
i'm fragile
and i'd like to stay that way

don't waste tears that are
shed
water your flowers with them
instead

the world is
loud
I can't hear
myself think

When you left
You took all I had with you
Dreams
Hope
Happiness

-Thief

The opposite of beauty is not ugly

How many breakups have you had?
It might be none, but I still know how it feels
to lose and be lost,
to love and be loved
to be held, and to be shoved
to fly and to fall
to hurt and be hurt

i'm either too much
or too little
i want to be a take what you can eat
but i know i am more of a sit down
than a buffet

-never 'just right'

I'm over you.

Or am i?

I'm finally free.

I thought I gave you up.

But shower thoughts suck me back in.

good

- i lied

How many times must
I disappoint
before it stops
hurting

How many times do
I have to cry
before my eyes
dry out

When will I find
expectations
too hard to live
up to

When will I decide
I might as well
give up

I wish I could make you smile
when you need me to
I wish I could say
the things that
you need to hear
and erase your worries
because even when nobody can see it,
I can feel it
And I just want you to
know that it'll be okay

i'm sorry

 -just pray

It's my own fault I appear so dull and drab and spiritless
It's my own fault you don't know the real me
It's my own fault I fell so deeply into this trap

 of plain

It's my own fault I can't escape

I've been in love
Was it real
I thought so…
But how am I supposed to know
Is there harm in trying
Will the band-aid no longer stick
after being ripped away another time

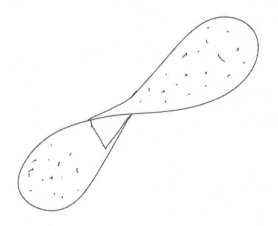

Your rhyme and rhythm was my theme song
But I hear it through different ears now
What once was a great symphony of sounds
Has morphed into a chorus of lies

cry here

i'm sorry.
this too shall pass
you are loved

you're still living our ten year-old dreams
it's just that i'm not in them anymore
-replaced

I won't allow to be loved partly
I need wholehearted or not at all.
If you don't love all of me with all of you
I can't trust any of it.

If you want me to improve
you'll have to do more than
criticize my moves
If you actually want me to make a change
don't just laugh at the way I am

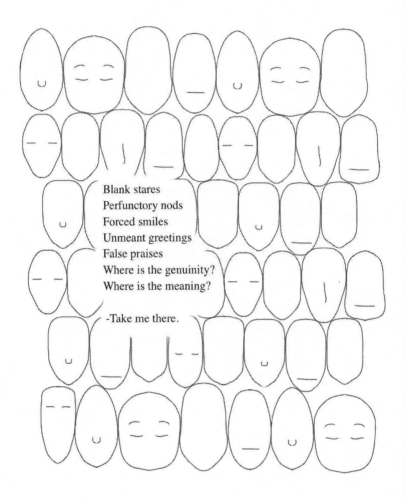

Blank stares
Perfunctory nods
Forced smiles
Unmeant greetings
False praises
Where is the genuinity?
Where is the meaning?

-Take me there.

You used to walk with me
Hand in hand.
Now you act like I'm holding you back.

-Nothing to do but let go

what color represents you? he whispered
brown she said
a little bit of everything,
not enough of anything

you and I seemed like
we would line right up
but there were parts of you i didn't see
parts of you that were just right for her,
not me

it's rotten now.
we are rotten.
but i still have the sweet aftertaste
of what we had
lingering on my tongue.

you are the moon.
you stand by the sun and get credit for its vibrance

I'm starting to despise that look you give when I say their name
as if they're rotten
and not a human being

You were a weight around my ankle.
No, there wasn't anything wrong with you.
Just how you were attached.
Too closely.
I was always tripping over you
and you mistook it for kicking.
That's why I had to cut you off.

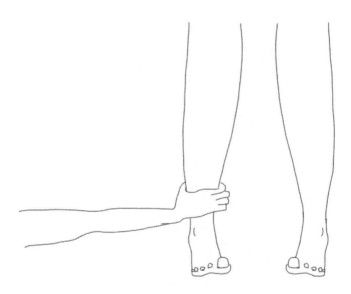

Lost civilizations
We destroyed them
Imagine what they could've become
Better than us, no doubt
We didn't even give them the chance
When they fought back
we called them evil
savages, uncivilized, unholy, uncultured
Imagine the wonders we could have had
And now we'll never know

were you born with that mask?

-fake

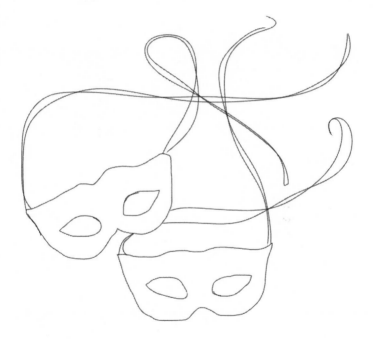

If you want me to change so badly
Why don't you say it to my face
And not the back of my head
or
hidden in glances

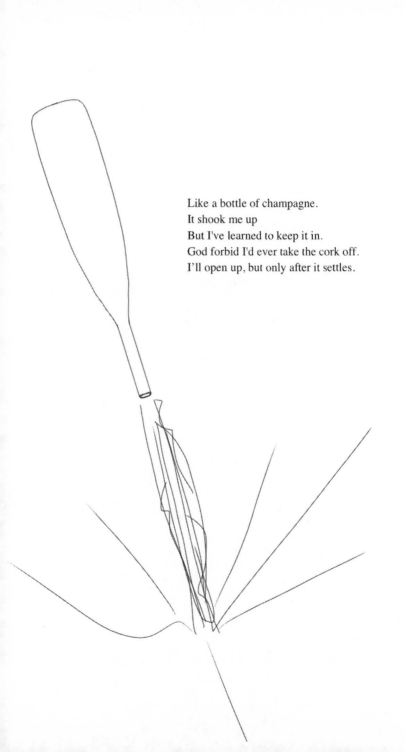

Like a bottle of champagne.
It shook me up
But I've learned to keep it in.
God forbid I'd ever take the cork off.
I'll open up, but only after it settles.

It might have ended
before it began
But I still feel hurt
and need to heal
from the invisible wounds

Does even one
understand my complexity?
My grooves, whiffs, whims
my strange ways
my late days?

Or will I simply be another
lost in translation?
Don't try to figure me out from a nip of a sentence,
to understand my thoughts
my fears, my life.
I'm afraid
if you do you'll
over simplify me like everyone else and I'll
be lost in translation.

Don't poke me down to IQ and GPA and stats
I have a purpose, a meaning,
a personality that spills
beyond the margins of my work.
I will not be

Lost in translation.

so many ways
so many types
the saddest kind is when they silently roll down your cheek
they come so naturally
don't take any effort
they just flow on their own

 -used to the tears

Not as glorious as a sunflower
Not as elegant as a rose
Not as peaceful as a lily
Not as wild as a daisy
But somewhere in between.

-I am a poppy

I worked hard to get here
took it step by step
surrounded myself with the right group
got myself on the right path
did things in the right order
And realized what is here
isn't what I want for myself.

pain comes in different colors

a rainbow
a spectrum of hurt
of misfortune

the way it comes out
shines through
leaks

anger is a burst of confetti
rejection is blurry blue eyes
loneliness is a burning white ache
regret is a heavy black heart

pain is beautiful
embrace its diversity

. . . LIVE

A balance of patching the leaks
and making more.
Of pondering and pushing limits
and learning to soar.

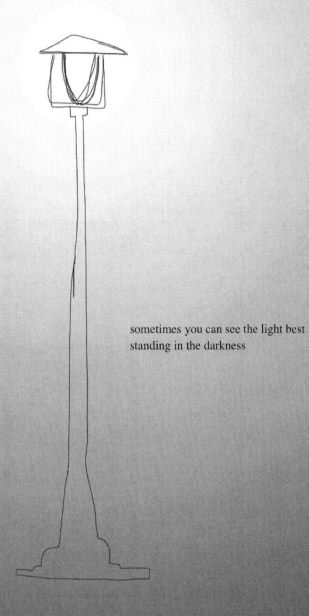

sometimes you can see the light best
standing in the darkness

just because at one point
i had bad
doesn't mean that now
i'll settle for moderate

they say beauty is pain
but out of pain comes beauty

yeah, i'm a mess
right now
but
watch out
let me get organized
and i'll
blow
your
mind

Don't let it break your heart.
Let it set your soul on fire.

Actually,
I think it's smarter to do
what I enjoy
More intelligent to surround
myself with good people
Wiser to hold on to
the big picture
Actually,
I think it's a brilliant idea
to be me

LORD, RELIGHT ME!
you gave me a wick for a reason!

it rushed over me like a breeze of warm air.
every setback that i've had
is simply a reminder
a reminder to come back to Jesus.
walking on the edge,
just shows me the drop
and i remember how much I need him
i so desperately need him.

If you want to win
stop playing.
If you want to prove you're stronger
let go.

If you have a problem
it's not new—God recycles
Someone has had it before
and made it through
If you don't think you can survive
I promise you someone before you
has made it out alive
Know that you are not alone
whatever you are going through
you can make it home
-God recycles

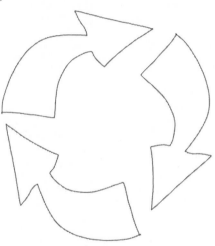

I want to be different
I want to be me
But I don't know what either
of those are yet
So here I am
in this awkward state of limbo
Trying to discover myself
and be myself
at the same time

-Who am I?

At least…
When I cry
When I'm sick to my stomach
When I'm so angry and frustrated
When I've got headaches
When I regret the things I did
and dread what I will do
When I've got aches and pains
Or when I drive myself mad
When I'm famished or exhausted
When I'm cold and dark
and in a bad mood
When I lash out
and don't mean the things I say
When I'm miserable
…I know I'm alive

negativity is contagious

-stay away from me

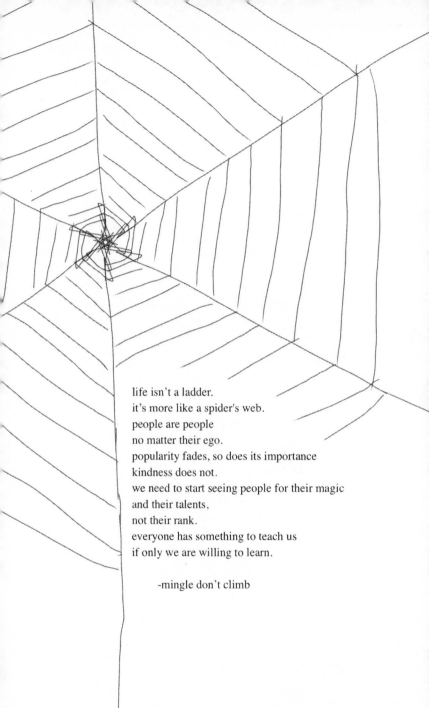

life isn't a ladder.
it's more like a spider's web.
people are people
no matter their ego.
popularity fades, so does its importance
kindness does not.
we need to start seeing people for their magic
and their talents,
not their rank.
everyone has something to teach us
if only we are willing to learn.

-mingle don't climb

155

I don't want to hear anyone say
oh well, it's life
Because life is what you make of it
Let's build the kingdom
instead of settling for a shack

we are

afflicted
but not crushed
perplexed
but not driven to despair
persecuted
but not abandoned
struck down
but not destroyed

we are

children of God

-2 corinthians 4:7

i can't believe i get to live in such an amazing time as the present
all these amazing people
and i get to live among them
it is thrilling to think i get to be amidst all the wonders of this planet
what if this is heaven and i'm just living in it?
how can i be so lucky?
it truly is spectacular
simply being alive

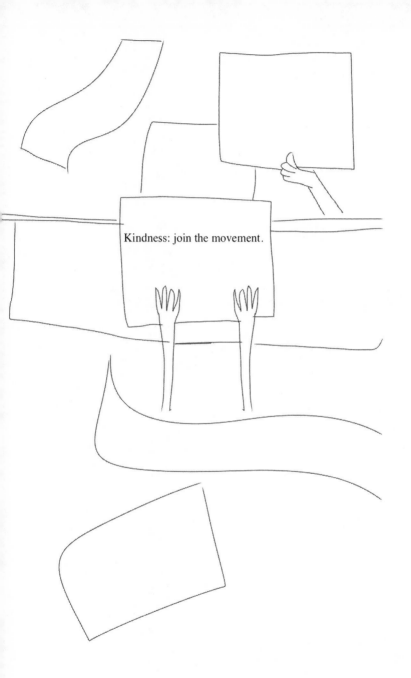

Kindness: join the movement.

We're building bridges
Diversifying the mind
Traveling beyond the normal
We are learning new cultures
As they learn ours

-world peace

she was like stained glass
made up of different colored parts
each piece reflecting a part of her soul.
people glance at sections and think she's confusing
but I dare you, take a step back.
all the little pieces make a beautiful masterpiece.

you hover outside my window
looking in
if only for a second
to tell me it's alright
  look at me
  i'm beautiful
  see my wings
  my feathers
  my sheen
not everything in this world is
darkening
losing its gleam

flyaway hairs dancing chaotically in front of my eyes
nothing but open road and
a full heart drowning in limitlessness fresh air
each breath propelling life into my being
not a care in the world

    -free

the body you are born in
doesn't matter
as much as how you create your soul.

Teach me to say
Lord willing

I don't want to fight You
I want to follow You

What You have planned for me
Is much better than whatever I've planned for myself

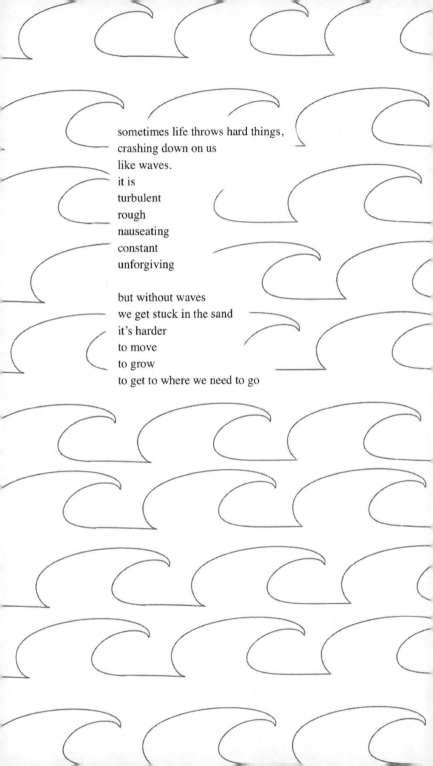

sometimes life throws hard things,
crashing down on us
like waves.
it is
turbulent
rough
nauseating
constant
unforgiving

but without waves
we get stuck in the sand
it's harder
to move
to grow
to get to where we need to go

I should have worried more
fretted over things that
might've mattered
Spent more countless hours
with a dead weight in my stomach
dreading each day to day

  -said everyone never

You can't control whether or not people like you,
but you can be a friend

  or not

You can't make people see you,
But you can be visible

  or not

You can't make people hear you,
but you can be loud

  or not

You can't make people follow you,
But you can be a leader

  or not

She thinks I'm better than her.
        I think she's better than me.
She thinks that I hate her.
        I think that she hates me.
That is how we feel it's been and
going to be. Imagine
if we could
overcome this thing of jealousy.
If we could
be friends and not enemies.

listen all the way through first
silence to silence on either side
listen to the beat
and the bass
and the harmony
listen to the melody
but don't tone out the strings
listen to the vocals
and sound effects
to the interludes and bridges
listen to the tremolo
and vibrato
listen to the things music has yet to name.
listen to the song

And if you still hate me, fine

oh
to be tied to the moment
as much as my thoughts are to every second of my future

-aspirations to be present

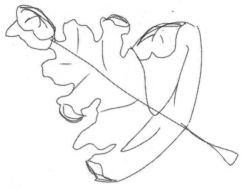

fall is soft smiles
grandma's knitted sweater
fall is pressing snooze on your alarm
enjoying the little things.
fall is looking downs and smiling at the legs you haven't shaved
fall is way too many chia tea lattes
and long, long hair.
fall is hikes
fall is puppy walks
fall is long talks with your friend
and cozy coffee shops
fall is looking back.
but mostly fall is being present

-appreciating

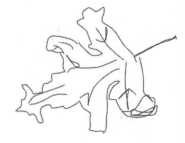

a glance.
maybe a little too long
a smile.
maybe a little too big
thoughts.
maybe a little too often

-crush

Pretty is the physical qualities you were born with
Perceptions of pretty change every day
But beauty is a kind heart.
A loving action
A brave defender

   -beauty is constant

I will always remember
the carefree times we had
in the orange glow of
flashlight under sheets
our faces made funny
by the deepening shadows
How our heartbeats rushed
each time we laughed for
the chance of being caught
only made us more crazed
with the induced high of
togetherness and nighttime

I need to read a book again
I haven't in a while
Haven't donated my soul
to the cover page page page cover rhythm
Those tightly wound words
haven't captured my attention recently
I haven't had the rollercoaster ride
I haven't felt the soaring highs
and aching lows
Haven't been a victim to the character's feelings
or longed to be standing next to them

why are we so worried
about what's real, what's not
what's accepted, what's not
I walk to my own beat
I sing to my own song

between her brows were the lines of worry
but even deeper were the lines around her mouth
holding memories between their folds
revealing shadows of her smiles
every freckle, every scar,
they all tell a story
a beautiful story of adventure
of strength and of hope
     -love your story

i am thankful
to be raised in joy and hope
and not doubt and judgment
taught to see good in all
so that when i meet them
i will see them for their strengths
for what makes them shine
you call it foolish

but i thank God
that i can look at a rock
and find the gold

i will never be a meanwhile
a just because
a why not
a no harm done
i have intentions of forever
or nothing

Come check me out
I dare you
Look past
these walls that I was born into
Look beyond
these bars,
this cage

This bird was made to fly

the stronger person shows their weaknesses
they're no longer afraid of
what others may do with them
they know their foundation won't topple
and revealing secrets
just fills the holes in the mortar

You can sleep when you're dead,
they said.
But if all I do is work,
it's as if I never lived

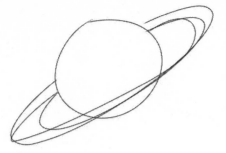

You are everything
and
You are nothing

You matter
and
You don't

To live a balanced life
You've got to have perspective

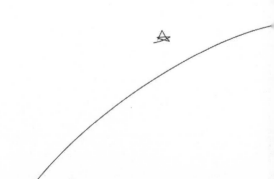

i see that everything in the past
happened exactly the way it was supposed to happen
how can I doubt God isn't doing the same now?

-trust the process

keep your heads on
it'll be alright

don't stop living now
you can't save these years
and hide them away for later

i'm sinking

calm my soul.
guide my steps.
clear my path.
help me rise above

over and over
on repeat

   -today's mantra

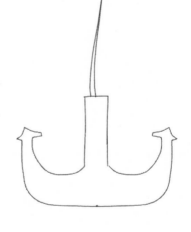

i want to be Jesus high
not worldly high
i want to be overflowing with his love
not keep it to myself
i want to be preaching through my actions
not just words
joyous,
not situationally happy

Even though they may be different
I try to wear my values like a crown

the sweet taste of progress lingers on my lips
all those slammed doors
have given me options
and those setbacks
have helped me grow
it was like they said
it truly does get better in the end

No longer will I run from my problems.
Happiness is a choice
and I've made it mine.
I can't avoid everything
so I will choose how I feel about it.
I have that control.
If it's all that's left,
I'll still be happy.

it's a passion
when i do it
i'm immersed
so immersed
it's like a glimpse into the future

Dream all night
Do all day

   -go get 'em

take a breath

get up

rock it

repeat

at breaking point
i usually realize i am more flexible than i thought

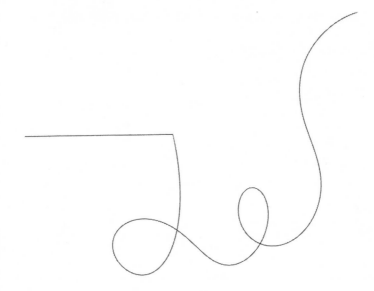

The ideas they have of me may be wrong
but I'm strong
The way they treat me may be careless
but I'm fearless
The things they do to me may be done
but I've won

Let God seep
Into your life.
Into all the broken areas
That you have given up on.
That you have let go of.
forgotten. abandoned.
Let him form you into
Who you aspire to be.

    -Kintsugi

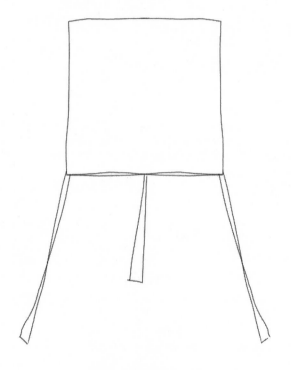

what you're about to write
deserves a fresh page
who you're about to become
deserves a blank slate

joy!
joy!
never knew it until now
it's different than happy
better than happy
i've been that before–
happy is the effect of something,
but this is different

-unspeakable joy

and now we conclude our collection of poems
strings of thought

thank you for joining us on this journey, and helping us
see that this cracked glass is a beautiful vase from which
our sweetest memories and hardest lessons bloom
into flowers.